PLEASE WASH YOUR HANDS BEFORE YOU READ ME AND KEEP ME CLEAN

For Arielle,
and for Chiqui too
D. S.

For Craig
T. H-N.

First U.S. edition 1994
Published in Great Britain in 1994 by Walker Books Ltd., London.

Library of Congress Cataloging-in-Publication Data

Sheldon, Dyan.
Love, your bear, Pete / by Dyan Sheldon ; illustrated by Tania Hurt-Newton.—
1st U.S. ed.
Summary: Although she misses her stuffed bear after he is
left behind on the bus, a young girl enjoys the post cards he sends her
from all the faraway places he visits.
ISBN 1-56402-332-X
[1. Lost and found possessions—Fiction.   2. Teddy bears—Fiction.]
I. Hurt-Newton, Tania, ill.   II. Title.
PZ7.S54144Lo   1994
[E]—dc20   93-2883

10 9 8 7 6 5 4 3 2 1

Printed in Italy

The pictures in this book were done in acrylic paints.

Candlewick Press
2067 Massachusetts Avenue
Cambridge, Massachusetts 02140

love, your Bear pete x

Dyan Sheldon

illustrated by
Tania Hurt-Newton

CANDLEWICK PRESS
CAMBRIDGE, MASSACHUSETTS

Brenda left her bear on the bus. His name was Pete. "Pete!" screamed Brenda, as the bus pulled away. She tugged her mother's arm. "Look! Pete's still on the bus! Let's run after him!"

But Brenda's mother wouldn't run. "Maybe someone will hand him in at the lost and found office," said Brenda's mother. "We'll have to wait and see."

Brenda started to cry.

Brenda finally stopped crying when her mother called the lost and found office. "Is he there?" asked Brenda. "Has someone turned him in?"

But no one had turned in a small blue bear with one black eye, one green eye, and one and a half ears.

"Did you tell them he's wearing a checked jacket?" asked Brenda. "Did you tell them he likes sleeping on his back?" Brenda's mother nodded.

"He may still turn up," said Brenda's mother. "We'll have to wait and see." Brenda started to cry again.

Pete did not turn up in the lost and found office.

Brenda moped around the house all that day, and all the next.

She sat by the window, watching the buses go by.

"Poor Pete," said Brenda. "He's all by himself on a bus. I hope he's not too lonely."

"I don't think he's poor at all," said Brenda's mother. "I think he's a very lucky bear."

"Lucky?" said Brenda. "Why?"

"Why, because he's having an adventure," said Brenda's mother. "Not many bears get a chance to ride on a bus by themselves. I bet he's having fun."

"But I miss him," said Brenda.

"And I'm sure he misses you, too," said Brenda's mother.

"No he doesn't," said Brenda. "He's probably forgotten all about me."

Brenda continued to mope.

And then, on the third day, she got a postcard. It was a picture of Big Ben. It was from Pete.

Brenda ran to her mother. "Look!" she cried. "Pete's been to see Big Ben! He's even heard it chime!"

"He must have gotten on a different bus, then," said Brenda's mother. "What else does Pete say?"

Brenda turned the card over.

"'London's very crowded,'" read Brenda, "'but I'm lonely without you. I wish you were here to hold my hand. Love, Your Bear Pete.'" Brenda looked at the picture again.

"I wish I were there, too," she said.

The next postcard Brenda got was from Paris.

"Paris!" exclaimed Brenda's mother. "I didn't even know Pete spoke French."

Brenda held up her postcard. "Look!" she said. "It's a picture of the Eiffel Tower. Pete went all the way to the top! He says it made him dizzy."

"What else does he say?" asked Brenda's mother.

Brenda read from the card. "'Having a wonderful time seeing the sights. If you were here we could go for a bike ride along the river. Love, Your Bear Pete.'"

"It sounds like he's having fun," said Brenda's mother.

"But it would be more fun if I were with him," said Brenda.

The next postcard
came from Venice.

"What a pretty
picture," said Brenda's mother.

"Pete went for a ride in a
gondola," said Brenda. "He ate a
lot of of ice cream and he bought
himself a straw hat. He says I'd like
the gondola. *And* the ice cream."

"What else does he say?" asked
Brenda's mother.

"'Remember when I fell in the
bath? I wish you were here to pull
me out if I fall in the canal. Love,
Your Bear Pete.'" Brenda looked
worried.

"I'm sure he won't fall in,"
said Brenda's mother.

"Pete hates getting
wet," said Brenda.
"If I were there I
could make sure
he didn't."

Brenda never knew
where Pete might
turn up next.

One day he might be in Mosco[w]

or Nairobi.

The next he might be in Cairo

or Tangier.

"I'll say one thing for Pete,"
said Brenda's mother.
"He certainly gets around."

Brenda
gazed out of
the window
and sighed.

"I wonder
what he's
doing now,"
she said.

"Maybe he's riding a camel past the pyramids.

Maybe he's buying fruit in a busy market."

"Maybe he's thinking of how it would be if you were there, too," said Brenda's mother.

Brenda got a postcard from Beijing.

"From China!" cried Brenda's mother. "What's Pete doing in China?"

"He's flying kites and eating with chopsticks," said Brenda.

"What else does he say?" asked Brenda's mother.

Brenda smiled. "'No one flies a kite as well as you do. And I wish you were here to help me with the chopsticks. I'm not getting very much to eat. Love, Your Bear Pete.'" Brenda stared at the card.

"We could fly a kite like a dragon, if I were there," said Brenda.

"That certainly is a very
unusual picture," said
Brenda's mother. "Where
on earth is Pete now?"

"He's in the Amazon
Jungle," said Brenda.
"He says it's very noisy
because of the parrots."

"It's just as well he doesn't
have two ears then," said Brenda's
mother. "What else does he say?"

"'There are lots of strange sights
in the jungle, but you wouldn't like
the bugs. It's a little scary without
you. Love, Your Bear Pete.'"

Brenda stared at the postcard.

"Oh, Pete," said Brenda. "If I were
there, we could sleep in a hammock
under the trees, and I'd hold you
very tight."

"And where is this from?" asked Brenda's mother. "That certainly doesn't look like the Amazon Jungle."

"It isn't," said Brenda. "It's the Grand Canyon. Pete rode all the way to the bottom on a mule. He found a feather on the trail."

"Imagine that," said Brenda's mother. "What else does he say?"

"'I wish you were here to sit around the campfire. Wouldn't it be nice to stay up all night and count the stars? Love, Your Bear Pete.'" Brenda shook her head.

"Pete can't count very well on his own," said Brenda.

Every morning, Brenda ran to the front door to get the mail. But one day there was no card. "Oh, no," wailed Brenda. "Pete has forgotten all about me!"

"What's this, then?" asked Brenda's mother. She held up a brown parcel. Brenda wiped a tear from her eye. "Is it for me?" she asked. "It has your name on it," said Brenda's mother.

Brenda tore off the wrapping.

Inside was a small blue bear with one black eye, one green eye, and one and a half ears, wearing a checked jacket, a straw hat with a feather in it, and a pin of the Eiffel Tower.

"It's Pete!" cried Brenda. "He's come back!"

In Pete's left paw was a very small chopstick and a bright purple flower. In Pete's right paw was a note.

"What does it say?" asked Brenda's mother.

Brenda read the note. "'It was a nice adventure, but I missed you too much, and I'm glad to be home. Love, Your Bear Pete.'"

"I'm glad you're home, too," said Brenda.

She gave him a hug.